DEDICATION

This book is dedicated to my daughters, Emma and
Brooklyn, who inspired me to write it.
And to my husband, Brian, for his love and support
throughout this process.

D1738544

Chapter 1

I was nine years old when my mother was diagnosed with cancer. The doctors told her she had maybe six months. My mother was never one to put much stock into the opinions of doctors; so she said she had decided to live longer. She did. She died three days after my thirteenth birthday. During those last few years she spent a great deal of time writing. At the time, I didn't know what she was writing. I guess maybe I was afraid to ask. On my thirteenth birthday I found out what all the writing was about.

For my thirteenth birthday my mom gave me her jewelry box. As I opened the jewelry box the scent of

Dear Anna,

By Jami Brookes Berry

my mother's perfume filled the air, a scent that over time would gradually fade, but never go away completely. Inside I found that the jewelry box was packed full of envelopes. Each had an event written on the front: The Day You Turn Sixteen; The Day You Graduate from High School; The Day You Get Married. She had written me a letter for every event that she could think of that she knew she was going to miss. It was a bitter sweet moment. I was so happy to have a piece of her that would stay with me throughout my life, but I knew how close we must be to the end for her to give this to me. Three days later I said goodbye to my mom.

The day my mother passed away I went into my bedroom, opened the box and took out the first envelope: The Day I Leave You.

Dear Anna,

I want you to know how much I love you. Right now I know that you are going through so much pain and I want nothing more than to be able to be there and hold you and tell you that everything will be okay. Of all the letters that I've written to you, I wrote this one the very last because the thought of leaving you has been more painful to me than any of the other things I've been through the last few years.

Through it all, the hardest part has been knowing that I would not be around to see you live your life. I spent many hours thinking of all the things I would say to you at the pivotal moments in your life.

That is why I wrote you these letters. I want to be with you. I want you to be able to read these letters, hear my voice in them, and know that I am always with you. I am watching over you. I don't know exactly how things work on the other side, but I feel certain that in the next life I will get to watch you live your life.

I know that this is hard for you, but know that I am free now. Free from the pain that I have felt for so long. Just think of me in heaven, dancing the way we used to dance around the living room, finally feeling whole and well again.

Anna, life will be hard, that I can tell you. Life comes with so many challenges, so much pain, but there is so much beauty to be had. There is so much love and joy. Don't let the pain of loss overshadow the good in life.

Live your life! Learn from your mistakes. Experience all the joy, the pain, the wonder that this world holds. Don't live a life full of "what ifs." One of my greatest accomplishments is being able to look back on my life and know that I had no regrets. I made many mistakes, but I wouldn't change a single one, because they shaped me into the person I became. I learned from them.

Be kind. There is already so much unkindness in this world; it needs more beautiful people like you. Never stop looking for the best in people. That is a quality of yours that I have always admired. You see in people what they do not even see in themselves.

Take care of your dad. He needs you more than he's willing to admit. He's a stubborn man, so he'll have trouble accepting help from others, but he'll need a lot of help from you.

When life becomes hard and seems unbearable remember that God is there for you. Pray and he will give you comfort, strength and peace. He will never leave you alone.

I love you. I miss you already, just writing this. I will

*always be with you. Please continue to talk to me. I'll always
listen. I love you. I love you.*

-Mom

Chapter 2

My mother always loved to garden. Our yard was carefully landscaped with flowers and plants that my mother had chosen over the years. In the middle of her flower garden was a large tree with a beautiful wrought iron bench underneath it. I remember sitting on it with my mother when I was small and listening to her recite my favorite books from memory. When I got older I would sit on that bench with her when I got home from school and tell her all about my day.

The day of my mother's funeral was long and draining. When it was over and all the family had gone home I found myself in the backyard, sitting on the bench. I ran my fingers over the intricate design on the bench and thought of all the times my mother and I had sat on this bench and talked and as I sat I found myself talking to her again.

"Mom, I miss you so much. Thank you for the letters. I've only opened the one, so far, but it has helped a little. I've probably read it a million times already. I miss you."

I sat there feeling a little bit self-conscious about talking to myself, but as I sat a breeze made the daisies dance and bob. The smell of the flowers reminded me so much of my mom that I could almost feel her there with me. I smiled to myself and walked back inside.

Over time the bench became the place where I went to talk to my mom. I would sit and tell her about my day or about how dad was doing. I'd update her about my friends and tell her all my thoughts and feelings. I didn't tell people about it, not even my dad. It was such a personal thing, so I waited until I was alone to talk to her.

The next letter that I read was one that I would end up reading over and over again throughout my life. When I first read it I couldn't even begin to imagine how many times I would read it and how much it would really help me. In fact, not long after reading it for the first time, I decided to make a copy of it, because I was worried about wearing out the original.

I opened the letter just a few days after my mother's funeral. The reason for reading it may seem trivial to anyone who has not lost someone close to them, but it was because a lady at the grocery store was wearing the same perfume that my mom always wore.

This familiar scent, which still lingers on the letters from my mother, was comforting in my own home, in my own room, when I chose to bring on the memories that came rushing back at the slightest whiff. But there was something jarring about those memories flooding back at the store. I almost felt as though the whole store could suddenly see all the pain that I was going through; as though my mother's passing had left a visible hole in me.

That night when I was alone in my bedroom I opened the box of letters, just to smell her perfume again. That's when I discovered that not every letter from my mom was for a specific date or event in my life. The envelope that was on the top of the pile said simply: When Life Is Hard.

Dear Anna,

I'm sorry that you're going through a hard time right now. I may not know now all the hard things that you are going to have to endure throughout your life. The truth is that life if full of challenges and the answer on how to handle each differs, but there are some things that I have learned about facing life's challenges.

Trials are a part of life and I've always believed that there is purpose in all things. Every experience that we have in life teaches us something. It's easy to begin to feel picked on. It is easy to ask, "Why me?" But questions like that get you nowhere. Often there are no answers, at least not in this life, as to why we are called upon to face certain challenges.

Know that no matter what you may be facing you are not alone. You have family and friends who love and care for you. You have a mother who is watching over you.

Pray and you will be guided and comforted through anything you may have to endure. It's okay to have moments of doubt or fear. There will be times when you feel like you can't stand anymore and that you are being tried beyond what you can bear. When that happens, pray harder. In my experience, the trials are not removed; the problems don't dissolve or become less complicated, but you are blessed with strength beyond your own.

Life is beautiful. Look for the beauty, despite whatever you may be going through. I miss you. I love you more than words can express.

-Mom

Chapter 3

It was a couple more years before I opened a new letter. The truth is that some days there was a part of me that wanted to just sit down and open up every envelope, to soak up as much of my mom as I could. But the other part of me wanted to wait; to stretch what I had left of my mom out as long as I could.

I often reread the two letters that I'd already opened and I spent a lot of time on our bench talking to mom. Each time I read them something different seemed to stand out to me, depending on what was going on in my life. And each time I read them, I could almost hear her voice. I could imagine the inflection that she would have used in her voice, if she had been reading them to me.

Despite the passage of a couple of years, the pain of losing my mother still seemed so new and so intense. My dad and I did our best to comfort each other, but my mother's passing had taken a piece of each of us. And when someone hurts that badly I don't know that they can really help someone else deal with their grief as well. But we tried, and there was a certain comfort in simply knowing that someone else knew how much it hurt; that someone else felt the same emptiness that my mother's passing had left behind.

There were moments when I forgot that she was gone. Not in a good way, like I was enjoying myself so much that I forgot, but in a very painful way.

It usually happened right when I woke up, before I was fully awake, and part of me would expect to see my mom poke her head in my room or hear her humming in the shower. Then I'd remember that she was gone and it was like it would suddenly hurt all over again.

The morning that I read the third letter was not one of those mornings, though. I had taken the letter out of the box the night before and set it on my nightstand. I had set my alarm clock and gone to bed; though the anticipation of opening another letter actually kept me awake for a long time. I apparently did fall asleep eventually because I woke up to the sound of my alarm clock early the next morning: at 3:49 AM, the exact minute I was born. I sat up, turned on the lamp and picked up the envelope: The Day You Turn Sixteen.

Dear Anna,

I can't believe you're sixteen years old today. It seems like just yesterday I was holding you in my arms for the first time and now you're a young lady. I can just imagine now what a beautiful young woman you'll be.

I know that the teenage years can be very hard. There's a lot of pressure to be what people want you to be. Friends will try to tell you what to like. Some people will tell you that you need to change this or that about yourself. But, know that you are beautiful just the way you are.

I know that when you're sixteen years old boys and friends seem like the most important things in the whole world, but keep a good perspective. High school isn't easy. There will be times when friends do things that hurt you and boys may break your heart, but please remember that it doesn't last forever. Life goes on and it only gets better as you get older.

You'll be starting to date soon and I know that it can be exciting and scary all at the same time. Just remember that dating is supposed to be fun. Spend your time with guys that respect you and respect your standards. Remember that no one that cares for you would ever ask you to lower your standards. Love and respect yourself and those around you will love and respect you too.

Enjoy being a teenager, while it lasts. Don't take things too seriously. There will be plenty of time later to fall in love and plan a life. Relax and enjoy the moments, because they'll be gone before you know it. Remember to protect your heart. Don't give it to anyone who isn't worthy of you.

Drive carefully, love cautiously and know that I am always there for you. I love you.

-Mom

Chapter 4

My mom was right about high school being hard. I think that my high school experience was probably similar to most people's experience. There always seemed to be drama. Most of it was just the normal high school stuff. My friends and I would get so worked up over whether or not we'd be asked to the latest school dance; I'd get stressed out over trying to pass a test at school. Looking back later I realized how trivial it all was, but at the time it all seemed to matter so much.

On top of the normal stress that comes with being a teenager, everything seemed intensified to me because my mom wasn't there. Sometimes I couldn't help thinking to myself, "Becky wasn't asked to the school dance either, but at least she has her mom there to talk to about it." So many things still reminded me that she was gone.

Most days I went through the same motions that everyone else at school did, but there were a handful of moments that seemed to set me apart as 'the girl who lost her mom'. The time that still stands out to me is when I had a substitute teacher that had known my mom years earlier. She recognized my name on the class roll.

"Are you Julia's Anna?" I managed to get out a weak, "Yes." But I couldn't even speak when she followed up by asking, "How is she?"

I'd gotten used to, "I was so sorry to hear about your mom," but this was a whole new pain. After what seemed like an eternity of silence I heard a voice behind me say, "She passed away a few years back."

I stood up and walked out of the room and out of the school. I got into my car. The tears started rolling down my cheeks. I sat in the parking lot and cried for the rest of the class period.

Overall, I still had many of the normal high school experiences. I failed a few tests. I made some friends and I lost some friends. I went to homecoming and to my senior prom. Most of my high school years were what I would call unremarkable and I was not exactly sad to see them end when graduation finally came around.

The day of my high school graduation went by slowly. The process of getting lined up and seated was monotonous. The speeches seemed to drag on forever. And the procession to shake hands with our principal and receive my diploma was tedious.

It was made worse by the fact that it wasn't even my real diploma, but a paper that had instructions on how and when to pick up the actual diploma. For me it was made even worse by a decision that I had made to wait until after the graduation ceremony to read the next letter from my mother. I had tucked it into my pocket, underneath my graduation gown.

After the ceremony was over, I snuck out a side door, climbed up a small hill, and sat down on the grass to open the envelope: The Day You Graduate From High School.

Dear Anna,

Congratulations! Graduating from high school is such a big step. I don't know about you, but for me the Graduation Ceremony seemed to drag on forever and I was ready to just be done and bolt out the door. But don't take this for granted, it only happens once. Take the chance to say goodbye to friends you've made. You'll be surprised how quickly you lose touch with people that you've seen every day for the last few years.

Graduating from high school also means making some adult decisions. It can be exciting and scary all at the same time. Don't let other people influence you in making decisions on where to go to college or what to major in. Follow your own dreams. Be who you want to be.

I know that you may be feeling like you need to stay home and take care of your dad, but don't let that stop you from going where you want to go. He would never want to think that he held you back from what you really wanted to do.

I don't know what may have happened in the last few years. For all I know you may have dreams of running off to Broadway or Hollywood and becoming some big star. No matter what your dream is now, an education is very important. Please don't put off getting a good education. It will help you throughout your life no matter what you choose to do.

I am so proud of everything that you have done to get where you are now. I love you.

-Mom

Chapter 5

After graduating from high school I certainly had no dreams of Broadway, Hollywood or stardom, but my mom had definitely been right about one thing; I was hesitant to leave my dad. In the years since my mom's passing my dad had never started dating again.

Some of our relatives had tried to tell him that he needed to move on and meet someone new, but my dad just wasn't interested. I once heard him ask my aunt Deb how he could go out and date other people when he still loved my mom every bit as much as when she was alive; it's hard to argue with that.

I worried about abandoning him and leaving him alone, so I began looking into my options at the local community college. I still didn't know for sure what I wanted to do with my life, so I rationalized that starting at the community college was the most practical choice anyway.

My friends were all going in different directions. Some were staying; some going off to different colleges throughout the state and a couple of them were leaving the state altogether. One of my friends said she was taking a year off to travel and "find herself". Her parents were apparently willing to pay for such a discovery, because they were footing the bill. I laughed about the cliché of it all, but part of me longed for that kind of freedom; to be able to go somewhere else, somewhere that no one knew me.

I applied to different colleges, mostly just to give the appearance of weighing my options, and I applied for scholarships, too. My grades had always been good and I had tested very well on the SATs. And I guess that part of me wanted so badly to go away to college that I thought maybe if I got a good enough offer it would push me into going; maybe I'd get an offer that was too good to refuse and I'd feel like I just had to take it.

What I got were a few offers that were too good to refuse and yet I still couldn't pull myself away from my dad. I never said this to him and I never showed him the scholarships that I was being offered. But then one day my dad asked over breakfast, "So have you decided where you're going to school?" I told him about the community college and talked it up big like I was excited. He set down his spoon and looked me in the eye and said, "It's okay to leave. I'll be okay."

I hesitated. I knew he meant it, but I just wasn't sure how he would be okay without me; or how I would be okay without him, for that matter. But I realized that sooner or later I would have to move on and live my own life. He and I talked about the options that I had. A few days later I mailed off a letter accepting an offer for a scholarship from a school that was two hours from home.

That fall my friend Jenny and I got into her car, the trunk and back seat stuffed full of all of our things, and headed away to college together. On my lap was the jewelry box and I clung to it tighter as I watched my dad, standing on the front porch, get smaller and smaller as we drove away. Jenny and I had found a basement apartment off campus with two bedrooms. That night as I sat in my new room, I opened the box and pulled out the next envelope: The Day You Leave for College.

Dear Anna,

I know that you are probably feeling a whole mix of emotions right now. I'm sure that you are excited to be on your own and probably a little nervous too. I imagine it's probably hard on you, leaving your dad behind. I know that he understands, Anna. At some point you had to move on and live your own life.

College is such an exciting time. Take the time to go to your classes and study and really learn while you're in school. I know it's easy to get caught up in the social aspect of college and while that is part of the experience, don't let your education suffer because of it.

I don't know if you've decided what you want to do with your life yet, but if you're anything like I was you probably have no idea, really. Let me give you some advice, find something you love to do and do it. I remember putting so much consideration into how much a certain field might pay and then I'd start down the road for that major and discover that I hated every class and I'd change my major again and again. Finally I realized that nothing can compare with doing something that you love for a living.

Even though your education is important allow yourself to take a break and socialize once in a while, too. Don't worry too much about meeting someone at college. I knew girls at school who seemed to be majoring in trying to find a husband and they spent most of their time miserable trying to "make it happen" for them. Enjoy college and if you happen to meet someone special, then great, but if not, it will happen when the time is right.

Have fun, study hard and know that I love you.

-Mom

Chapter 6

Being two hours from home at college also meant being two hours away from the bench in the garden. The first few weeks of school I found myself missing my mom even more, because I hadn't yet found a place to talk to her. It may seem silly, but it had always felt like I was closer to her and I could talk to her more easily on that bench.

Three weeks after school started I was walking past a park near my apartment when I noticed a tree at the far side of the park. The tree reminded me of the one in my mother's garden, so I went and sat underneath it and watched the sun set.

I leaned my head back against the tree and looked up through the branches at the pink and orange colors streaking across the sky. A breeze made the leaves sway and dance on the tree. And as I watched the leaves I found myself talking to my mom again.

This became my spot while I was away at college. I would usually come in the early evening and watch the sun set. I felt connected to my mom there, as though she was watching the same sky change colors as the sun ducked down behind the mountains. Maybe she was.

I told my mom about everything going on in my life. I told her about classes and friends and about the cute guy in my chemistry class. I smiled because I could almost hear her, always ready with a joke, retort, "So you guys have chemistry, huh?" I told her that his name was Mike and that he could make me laugh. Over time I told her all about him. But more importantly, I told him all about her.

Since my mother had died I had talked about her

very little and usually only with my dad. I had never actually even said her name aloud since she'd passed away. But Mike was special and I wanted to tell him everything. We would sit for hours talking about anything and everything, but somehow the conversation always came back to my mom.

I told him about how she could cook almost anything from scratch, but she always burned the cookie dough that came in a tube. I talked about how she brightened up a room when she walked into it and how she could always make me laugh, no matter what I was going through.

I told him about how she'd died and how much I missed her; how I still missed her. I told him about the box and the letters and I even told him about the tree in the park and the bench in the garden.

One day, after having heard just about every story I had to tell about my mom, he asked, "What's your mom's name?"

I took a deep breath before answering. "Julia," I finally said.

He smiled down at me, sitting with his arms around me, "It's a beautiful name. It would be a good name for a little girl." I smiled up at him, "Yeah. It's a beautiful name."

A few days later Mike took me to a concert at the school. Afterward we walked through a garden on campus talking and laughing.

Mike stopped and held my hands and told me how much he loved me. Then he pulled out a small box. He opened it. The ring sparkled in the moonlight. I said yes and he shakily slid the ring on my finger.

Afterwards, we sat in the garden and talked for hours until campus security passed by and kindly asked us to move along. It was late when I got home and I was excited and exhausted all at once, but I opened the box and pulled out the envelope that I had been anticipating opening for the last few weeks: The Day You Get Engaged.

Dear Anna,

I can't believe that my baby is engaged! It is such a fun and exciting time. I recommend a simple wedding and a short engagement. Your father and I were married four months after we got engaged and it seemed like an eternity.

Keep the wedding simple. It's easy to get caught up in dresses, food, flowers and all the latest wedding fads, but the thing that matters is that you are marrying the love of your life. Too much of all the other stuff can make you lose sight of that.

It can be stressful planning a wedding, even a simple wedding. Take time to still go out on dates and talk about things other than the wedding. Talk about the life you want to build together. Talk about your dreams and hopes for the future: the house you want to own someday, the family you want to have.

When it comes to your wedding plans, do whatever it is that you want to do and don't worry about what other people say. If what you really want is to serve soda and candy bars at the reception, then serve soda and candy bars. It's your day and it should be about you and your future husband.

I wish I could be there with you and help you plan everything. I can just imagine how beautiful you'll look in your wedding dress. (Don't feel like you need to wear mine, by the way.) I love you. I miss you.

-Mom

Chapter 7

We set a wedding date for three months after our engagement. It didn't leave us a lot of time for planning the wedding, but once we had decided that we wanted to be together forever, we didn't want to wait to get started. Mike and I started planning right away.

We picked out invitations and a cake. Mike and I decided to have an ice cream sundae bar for our reception and we found a little ice cream shop to cater the whole thing. I asked Jenny to be my maid of honor and she started helping me plan. She came with me to look at flowers and bridesmaid dresses.

With all the planning though, there was one part of the wedding that I put off planning as long as I could: the wedding dress. Ever since I was a little girl I had imagined shopping for my wedding dress with my mom. Going without her now seemed almost unbearable. Jenny offered to come with me, but taking someone else seemed worse, so I went alone.

I walked into the store alone and was greeted by the sales woman that my appointment was with. After a quick explanation that no one else was meeting me there, we started to look through some of the dresses in the store.

I pointed out things that I liked and things that I didn't like on different dresses. We pulled a few to try on, but nothing jumped out at me. After trying on the ones that we'd taken into the dressing room, the lady excused herself to go find some more dresses that I might like.

There was a picture of my mom that always sat on my dad's nightstand. It was a picture of her on their wedding day. Her wedding dress was stunning. It had long sleeves made of lace and little buttons running all down the back of the dress. Her dress didn't have a long train, but instead the skirt was actually cut mid-calf. I remember my mom telling me how upset her mother had been about the fact that her ankles were showing in her wedding dress.

The sales woman returned carrying four dresses. She opened one of the dress bags and I could see that this dress had little buttons running all down the back. As she pulled the dress from the bag I saw that it had no train. "Now this one is a little different," the lady was saying as she helped me pull the dress over my head, "The dress actually only goes to about mid-calf, but I thought you might like it; something kind of different."

I looked at my reflection in the mirror. It was by no means a duplicate of my mother's wedding dress. There were no lace sleeves and the overall style of the dress was more modern, but it was perfect.

After that, everything else fell into place with the

wedding plans. Time seemed to fly by, mostly because it was so packed with wedding stuff: sending out invitations, attending bridal showers, tuxedo fittings, dress fittings. Before we knew it we were into the last week of March: the week of our wedding.

We had decided that we would spend the night before the wedding alone with our own families and do something special with them one last time. It was Mike's suggestion and I think he really just wanted to give me some time alone with my dad. So, Mike and his family had pizza and family movie night at home and my dad took me out to dinner.

During dinner my dad handed me a small box. "I thought you might want to wear it tomorrow," he said, already tearing up. I opened the box and inside I found my mother's pearl necklace; the same necklace that she had worn to their wedding. My eyes filled with tears as I ran my fingers over the pearls and remembered all the times I had seen her wear it.

My dad lifted the necklace from the box, "May I?" I lifted my hair out of the way and he fastened the necklace around my neck.

"You look so much like her now."

"Really?" I asked.

"Of course. You're a beautiful . . ." he hesitated, "You're a beautiful woman."

I hugged him tightly, "Thank you, Daddy."

After dinner we went home and looked through old family photo albums. We talked about old times. We talked about mom, but not with the same pain and sadness that had always been there before. We remembered the good times. We laughed. It felt good to laugh with my dad again. It was a good night.

There was one letter in the box that was not addressed to me: To My Son-In-Law on the Day You Marry My Daughter. After reading it, Mike asked me if I wanted to read it too, but I told him, "No." That was his one and only tie to my mom and I wanted it to be his alone. Besides, I had a letter of my own: The Day You Get Married.

Dear Anna,

Of all the days that I regret not being there with you, I think this is the hardest of all. From the day you were born I imagined what it would be like when you got married. I imagined helping you get into your dress and placing your veil on your head. I imagined the beautiful woman that you would be.

I know that your wedding day can be exciting and stressful and scary all at once. Please take the time to savor those little moments today. Don't get so caught up in the details that you miss the important things.

Marriage can be hard at times. You will be blending two lives with completely different backgrounds and that won't always be easy, but as you work together you will figure out what things work for you.

Always tell each other, "I love you." That comes so naturally in the beginning, but can be easily forgotten as marriage becomes comfortable. Be kind to each other. Talk to each other; share your thoughts, your hopes, your dreams and even your fears. Let him see all of you. I know I told you before to protect your heart, but that's no longer your job, it's his job now. Give him your heart and let him protect it for you.

Anna, I can't tell you what your life will bring. I can't tell you how much time you will have together, but I can tell you that it will not be enough. At the end I wished that I had said, "I love you" more. I wished that I had held your father's hand more. When I hurt so much near the end I still asked your father to hold me, because I didn't want to miss a moment. Live your marriage as though your time together will be short. Forgive the little things. Dwell on what he does that makes you smile, not whatever little habits may drive you nuts.

Today you are marrying the person you love more than anything in the world. Don't forget how much you love him today. And just wait, it gets better still. As you grow together you will find that your love for him will grow, too. I love you and I'll be there with you today. I'm sure of it.

-Mom

Chapter 8

Our wedding was beautiful. The day was filled with family, friends and food. Looking back at it, I don't remember a lot of the details, but I remember the look in my dad's eyes when he saw me in the dress for the first time.

I remember the expression on Mike's face while we were being married. And I remember feeling my mom's presence there so strongly that I found myself looking over my shoulder as if I expected to see her sitting there along with the other guests.

After the wedding we spent the next day in our

one bedroom apartment opening presents and eating leftover wedding cake. The day after that we left on our honeymoon: a week-long trip to a lake side cabin.

When we returned from the trip, we settled into everyday life as a married couple. We worked, went to school, and enjoyed spending the rest of our time together.

The apartment that we were living in was small. The carpet looked like it was forty years old and the kitchen was straight out of the 70's. But we loved it because it was our first home and we did what we could to make it our own.

We started planning our life together. Mike had two years left of school to complete his Bachelor's Degree; I had three. But we both had good jobs and were working our way through school.

We decided that we wanted to start a family right away. We had already begun saving and should be able to buy a house in a year and a half. We figured we could make a one bedroom apartment work until then. We thought everything would work out great, just the way we planned.

The first few months of marriage were practically perfect. We never fought and we worked together well. Blending our lives really seemed like a piece of cake. I thought it was funny how so many people I knew had made a big deal about what an adjustment marriage was, because it seemed to be so easy for us, so natural.

But school got to be more stressful as finals were approaching. And as we tried to start a family and nothing happened, we both became more and more anxious. It was in the midst of all this tension that we finally had our first fight as a married couple. It was nothing really. Within an hour or so we had made up, but at that time it really seemed like a big deal.

I don't actually remember what the fight was about, something trivial I'm sure: whose turn it was to empty the trash or when to add the detergent to the washing machine, before or after the clothes, or something along those lines.

What it was about doesn't really matter, but it

really upset me. Part of me had actually believed that we loved each other so much that we would just never fight. I got so upset that I went into the bedroom and locked the door.

I knew that there was a letter from my mom for this exact occasion; I knew every envelope in that box. I had actually laughed a little when I had seen the envelope, thinking that maybe I'd never need it.

For some reason I didn't immediately open the letter. I guess I wanted to calm myself down before I read another one of my mom's letters.

Or maybe I was afraid that it would tell me to just swallow my pride and go apologize, like she used to tell me when I fought with my cousins. Finally I pulled down the jewelry box and pulled out the envelope: When You Have Your First Fight with Your Husband.

Dear Anna,

When I decided to write these letters I made a list of all the moments in your life that I thought you'd need me most. I thought back over my life and I remembered times that I had picked up the phone and called my mom for advice. This letter seemed a little silly to me, but I remember how much I needed to talk to my mom after the first fight I had with your dad.

I actually still remember that fight. We got into a little disagreement over how to load the dishwasher. Neither of us would concede that there might just be two ways to load a dishwasher and soon we were into a full-blown argument. I know it sounds ridiculous, but that's usually how the first fight starts.

I think the hardest part about the first fight as a married couple is it's the first time you realize that marriage is not always perfect; marriage isn't always bliss. For me it was when I realized that we would not always agree, but that's okay. Remember it was just a fight. It's not the end of the world, just the beginning of reality.

You probably both said some things that you didn't mean, or at least that you probably shouldn't have said. I'm sure you both have some things to apologize for.

Forgive each other and move on. There's very little in this

*life that is worth staying mad about. Remember how much you
love each other. I love you, Anna.*

-Mom

Chapter 9

Life went on, but things didn't go exactly according to plan. We each finished another year of school. Mike got promoted at work. There was still no baby. But with Mike's new promotion we were able to start looking for a house.

We looked at some beautiful houses, but each one seemed to have something that we didn't like: the yard was too small; it was too close to traffic; it needed too much work. One day Mike came home and told me about this house that he had passed on the way home from work that day. We had both taken to driving through random neighborhoods, looking for houses for sale.

We contacted our realtor and he set up a showing for the house. We walked through the house and it was absolutely beautiful. I loved the kitchen with tons of counter space. Mike was particularly fond of the man cave, pool table included. But when we stepped into the backyard, we knew. "This is our home," Mike said to me. I nodded.

The backyard reminded me of my mom's. There were flowers everywhere and a vegetable garden along the back fence. There were two huge trees, one on each side of the lawn. An arbor covered with vines and flowers stood at the gate to the front yard.

We made an offer on the house. I was naïve enough to think that we would make an offer and they would just accept it and we'd have a house. It didn't work that way. They made a counter-offer, but it was just more than we could afford. Mike and I talked about it and decided that our offer was as high as we could really go. We had to walk away from the house we loved.

We each put on a brave face and made reassuring comments to each other about how there were plenty of houses out there and we'd find one even better. I was heartbroken. I loved that house. I loved that yard. I had felt so sure that it was going to be our home. Two weeks later our realtor called us and told us the people selling the house had changed their minds and they were willing to accept our initial offer. We had a house!

We signed the pile of papers that come with closing on a house. After getting the keys to the house, Mike and I went about fixing some things up before moving in. We painted the house and replaced some things here and there. The day before we moved into the house, Mike said he had one last project to finish on the house. So he went to the house and I stayed at the apartment and finished packing boxes.

The next day, a few friends showed up early and we got everything packed and over to our new house. We unloaded the boxes and the furniture from the moving van and then treated everyone to lunch. Mike and I got back to the house after lunch and I sat down on the floor of the front room to start unpacking boxes. Mike reached down for my hand and pulled me back up, "First I have something to show you."

Mike led me through the kitchen and out the door, into the backyard. Sitting under one of the trees was a bench almost identical to the one in my mom's garden. Tears filled my eyes. I sat on the bench and Mike sat next to me. "It's my house warming present to you," he said and he handed me an envelope. He kissed me on the forehead and walked back into the house, leaving me alone with my thoughts.

I sat, silently for a moment. In the past year I hadn't taken much time to talk to my mom. So before I opened the letter I sat for a while and just talked.

I told her about how much all these letters meant to me and how I had reread some of them so many times. I told her about trying to start a family and how hard it was that it still hadn't happened for us. I talked to her for a long time and then I opened the envelope: The Day You Get Your First House.

Dear Anna,

Congratulations! Buying a house for the first time is so exciting! I know that it's easy to get caught up in what other people have and what you think your house lacks, but remember that this isn't just a house, it's your home. Be happy with what you have and don't be too focused on what you don't have.

I remember when your dad and I bought our house; we figured that it would be our starter house and that someday we'd buy something bigger or newer. In the beginning I would talk about how someday we'd have a house with this or that.

But time passed and I stopped looking at it as a house that didn't have enough storage space or that had a kitchen that was too small, and I started seeing it as the house where you took your first steps and the kitchen where I taught you to cook.

By the time we could afford to buy something else, we

didn't want anything else. It was our home.

Enjoy making your house into your home. I love you.

-Mom

Chapter 10

Gradually we made the house our own. I spent a lot of time in the garden; I finally understood what my mother had loved so much about gardening. Mike turned out to be quite handy around the house. He seemed to almost get excited when something around the house broke.

It was starting to feel more like our home, but something was still missing; the room that we planned would someday be a nursery was still nothing more than a storage room. I thought about clearing the boxes out of the room and putting them into the basement or the garage, but an empty room seemed even worse.

Time went on and Mike finished his Bachelor's Degree. With his degree he again got promoted at work. He was making enough now that I could quit work if I wanted, but I chose to keep working. I wanted more than anything to be a stay at home mom, but a stay at home wife didn't have quite the same appeal.

A couple of months later I sat, staring at the results of a pregnancy test for about the millionth time. I guess a part of me thought that it may have changed in the two minutes since I'd last looked at it. I still couldn't believe what I was seeing. Not one line, but two. We were pregnant!

I had thought that I was getting the flu. I'd been throwing up the last few days. I actually didn't think that I might just be expecting. Months ago I would have immediately jumped to that conclusion. When we decided to start a family we thought that it would just happen. At first we were excited, but as the months passed we both began to get more impatient and as a year passed and then another we became worried. We each wondered at one time or another if it was ever going to happen for us.

I'd gotten to the point that I wouldn't get my hopes up over little symptoms, so I had assumed that the throwing up was the flu. And the fact that I had eaten grilled cheese sandwiches with tomato soup for breakfast, lunch and dinner the whole week? Well that was probably the only thing that sounded good because of the upset stomach.

There was a part of me that thought, "Maybe, just maybe, this is it." But I didn't let myself think about it much, because I was still pretty certain that I'd just end up disappointed. I checked the test again.

Mike was just leaving work and I had managed to not tell him the good news when he'd called to say he was on his way. I wanted to tell him in a special way. Months ago I had secretly bought him a shirt that said, "World's Best Dad!" It was wrapped up and sitting on the dining table now.

I was so excited that I hadn't sat down since I

had gotten the test results. I paced around the front room waiting for Mike to get home. When I heard his key in the lock I practically ran to the door and threw it open before he'd even had a chance to turn the key. I rushed him in and plopped the present into his lap. When he opened it, he said nothing at first. Then he looked at me and just said, "Really?" I nodded, my eyes welling up with tears. He hugged me and we laughed and cried together.

We stayed in that night, watching a movie and eating the dinner that I'd made: grilled cheese sandwiches and tomato soup. That night before bed I opened the box and pulled out the envelope that I'd been waiting over two years to open: The Day You Find out You're Expecting.

Dear Anna,

Congratulations! Just the thought of you becoming a mom makes me smile from ear to ear. I know that you'll be a wonderful mother. Any child would be lucky to have you.

Pregnancy can be a very difficult, emotional time. From the moment you know you're expecting you begin to worry about everything. And I'm sorry to tell you that it's just the beginning. When you hold your baby for the first time the worrying doesn't stop.

Give yourself a break while you're pregnant. Don't worry so much about having a perfectly clean house or a four course meal for dinner. Do what's essential, but make taking care of yourself a priority. Keep in mind that you're busy making a person and that takes a lot of energy.

I love you and I hope that you have a very healthy and happy pregnancy.

-Mom

Chapter 11

At my first doctor's appointment everything looked good. We even got to hear our little baby's heart beat and see it pulsing on the ultrasound screen. We started to tell family and friends our good news. We were so excited it was hard not to blurt it out to everyone we passed on the street.

We started making plans for the nursery. We even moved the boxes to the basement; well, Mike did because he wouldn't let me lift a thing. We started talking about baby names. We both felt certain that we were expecting a little girl. There wasn't any science to back that up, just a feeling we both had.

Everything progressed normally and as we neared the twenty week mark the doctor set up an appointment for an ultrasound, to check the growth and development of the baby and to possibly find out if we were having a boy or a girl. Mike took the day off from work that day and we went to the appointment together.

The ultrasound technician was all smiles as she explained how the ultrasound would work and what she would be measuring. She squirted my stomach with the goo that is apparently so important to getting a good view during an ultrasound. As she started, she continued to chat with us, but then she became quiet. She set down the hand piece and excused herself to go get the doctor.

My heart felt as though it was going to pound out of my chest. Mike reached out and grabbed my hand. Neither of us said anything. We probably were only left waiting like that for less than a minute, but it seemed an eternity. The doctor came in the room and sat down next to me. She picked up the hand piece and began running it along my stomach. I desperately tried to make out something, anything on the screen, but I wasn't sure what I was supposed to be looking at.

The doctor set the hand piece down again and grabbed a wash cloth and handed it to me to wipe my stomach off. "I'm so sorry," she said to us, "there's no heart beat." I sat there, too stunned to speak. A moment passed in silence and then Mike asked, "Can you tell us if it's a boy or a girl?" The doctor managed a half smile, "It's a girl."

The doctor sent in another person to talk to us about what happened now. I don't think I said a single word the rest of the day. It was a few days later that I finally opened the one letter I had hoped never to have to read: If you Ever Have a Miscarriage.

Dear Anna,

I truly hope that you never have to read this letter. As

you know I had a miscarriage two years before you were born and so I know how painful it is. From the moment you find out that you are expecting, that baby is real to you and it doesn't make a difference if the loss comes early or later; I think it is still the same.

I wish there was something that I could say that would make you feel better, but there's really nothing that can fix this. Some well-meaning people will try. They'll say things like, "It's for the better, because something was probably really wrong," or "I'm sure things will turn out better next time." Remember that although those things only make you feel worse, those people don't mean to be insensitive, they just don't know what to say.

The truth is that there is nothing that they could say. Nothing anyone says can change the loss that you are experiencing. I don't know why you have to go through this. I wish I could take away the pain that you're going through right now.

Talk to your husband about what you're feeling. Grieve together and help each other through this difficult time. Don't rush into trying to get pregnant again too fast. Allow yourself *time to heal. Whenever you feel right about it, try again. And if you decide together that you just can't try again, that's okay too.*

When we lost Cameron I felt so angry and hurt and confused. I couldn't even imagine ever trying again. But time does have a way of dulling pain, at least enough to move on. I don't know how it all works, but I like to think that maybe Cameron was waiting for me on the other side.

I love you. I miss you. I wish I could be there for you.

-Mom

Chapter 12

It was a rough time for both of us, to say the least. I think only someone who has experienced a loss like that can truly understand how it feels, so having my mom's letter meant the world to me. I spent a lot of time in the garden reading and rereading that letter. I took comfort in the thought that maybe my mom was right, maybe Isabella Rose was now on the other side with my mom.

We tried to get on with life as best we could. I finished my final year of schooling. Mike and I took some time to travel together. We went camping in National Parks and visited sites of historical significance; that was Mike's idea of vacationing. For our fourth anniversary he took me to New York City and we attended a Broadway musical; my idea of a vacation.

When we got home Mike surprised me with a new puppy, a black lab. We named her Chloe. She followed me everywhere. She sat with me when I cried. It may sound odd, but having Chloe around really helped me heal.

A few months later, as we were getting ready for bed, Mike said, "I was thinking today that the basement seems pretty crowded. Maybe we should move some boxes up to the . . . the extra room."

The nursery had sat empty for over a year now. At first passing it had been a painful reminder and the door had remained closed most of the time. But recently I had begun to go inside again. The pain of what we'd lost was still there, but I had started to think about what could still be.

"I've been thinking about that room too," I said. Mike and I stayed up late talking about what to do with the room.

Two months later, the future of the room was a little more certain. We held off on telling anyone about our good news. We decided that I would quit my job and stay home. I didn't want to take any chances. We could only keep our news a secret for so long before I started showing. We told family and close friends; and anyone who was actually forward enough to ask.

We were excited, but part of me was still holding back. As we neared the middle of the pregnancy and scheduled the ultrasound, I got more and more nervous. When the day finally came I was terrified.

As I lay on the table, tears filled my eyes. The technician smiled at me, understandingly. Clearly she had been informed of the situation before hand. Mike was looking at me, perhaps unable to look at the screen. I closed my eyes and then I heard the rapid "thump, thump, thump".

"Good, strong heartbeat," the technician said smiling. I opened my eyes. I squinted at the screen.

I could see the little blip of the heart beating on the screen.

"Oh, my gosh," I said, choking up. I couldn't get anything else out. We watched as the technician pointed out different features: a hand, a foot, an arm. Sometimes I wasn't entirely sure what we were looking at, but I couldn't pull my eyes away: our baby. I felt so much relief knowing that we had made it past the point where we'd lost Isabella and the baby was still okay.

The technician pointed out the baby's profile and we could already see that the baby had Mike's pointy nose.

"Did you guys want to know if it's a boy or a girl?" the technician asked.

"Yes, definitely," Mike said. I just nodded.

"Let's see here. Looks like . . . it's a girl!"

Tears filled my eyes. I couldn't help remembering the doctor say those same words the last time we were here. But as I watched our little girl squirming and wiggling on the screen I pushed those thoughts from my mind and focused on this new little baby that we would be bringing home someday.

The first half of the pregnancy had seemed to drag on forever, probably because I spent it worrying so much. The second half of the pregnancy started to fly by. We started to get the nursery ready; we painted it pink and yellow. We bought a crib and my dad brought us the rocking chair that mom had rocked me in. There were baby showers and doctor appointments to keep me busy.

Time flew by until the last couple of weeks before my due date. Suddenly time seemed to practically stand still. I couldn't wait to meet our little girl; to hold her; to bring her home. I was getting impatient.

My due date came and went, and still no baby. I got more impatient. Mike was on edge, constantly. If I got up to use the bathroom in the middle of the night, he was out of bed, keys in hand, ready to go to the hospital, before I could even tell him it was nothing.

My doctor offered to induce me if the baby still wasn't here a week after my due date. We waited some more. We scheduled the induction.

The day before the scheduled induction my water broke. A very long twenty-two hours later our little girl was here: Elizabeth Julia. Lizzie. I held her in my arms; in awe. I was amazed by how much I loved this little person that I had just met.

She had Mike's nose, she had my lips and she had my mother's pale blue eyes. Everyone kept telling me that most babies' eyes start out light and they can change, but I insisted that they would stay that color. She was a beautiful baby.

I was exhausted. So was Lizzie. She ate a little and then fell asleep. Sleeping sounded so good, but before I could sleep I had Mike grab my bag and retrieve an envelope that I had been waiting to open for so long: The Day You Become a Mother.

Dear Anna,

I can't believe that my baby has a baby! It's crazy to me just thinking that this day will come. Having a baby is one of the most incredible experiences that you can have in life. I still remember the moment you were born. I remember holding my breath until I heard you cry. I remember holding you for the first time and just being overwhelmed by how much I already loved you.

My life changed the moment you were born. I started thinking about how everything would affect you. I started imagining your entire life; what you would do, what you would like, what kind of woman you would grow up to be. And I started to see myself through your eyes. I wanted to be the perfect mom. But the truth is there is no perfect mom.

Allow yourself to be imperfect. Don't worry about whether or not you're doing things right, just being there for your children matters more than anything else. Never question if you're good enough, because in a child's eyes no one is a better mommy than their mommy.

Don't be afraid to spoil your baby. Hold your baby as much as you can. Enjoy those moments now, because they will be gone before you know it and you will miss them more than you can possibly imagine.

Please tell your child about me. Tell them about how much Grandma loves them. I like to think that maybe I got to spend some time with them before they came to you. I like to think that they sat on my lap and I got to tell them what an amazing mom they were going to have. You will be an amazing mom.

I love you so much. Know that I am always with you.

-Mom

Chapter 13

After Lizzie was born I couldn't wait to take her home. I felt like I just couldn't get out of the hospital soon enough; we stayed two nights. The day we brought her home I was so excited and nervous. I sat in the back seat, next to her car seat, all the way home.

The first night home went well. Lizzie seemed like such a good sleeper; of course she was only a couple of days old. But within a week everything seemed to suddenly become harder. Lizzie wanted to be held all night long. I found it hard to get her to sleep even just two hours straight.

Mike and I took turns getting up with her; we were both sleep deprived. I looked online and in books trying to find something that would help her sleep. We tried everything we could find and nothing seemed to work. Mike and I kept reminding ourselves that someday we would actually miss this.

Lizzie wasn't even particularly unhappy. She wasn't like some babies that would scream and cry no matter what. She just wanted to be held, and as long as she was being held she was happy. Eventually she started sleeping more.

The first time she slept through the night we were awakened the next morning by the sun rising. We ran to the crib to make sure she was okay. She lay there peacefully sleeping, her chest gently rising and falling. We both climbed back into bed to take advantage of the chance to actually sleep.

From then on sleeping became less and less of an issue. She still had a restless night here and there, but for the most part she slept through the night. One night I just couldn't sleep and I snuck into the nursery. A little while later, Mike poked his head in and found me sitting on the floor next to the crib, watching Lizzie sleep. "She okay?" he asked.

"Yeah," I said, smiling sheepishly, "I couldn't sleep and I just missed her." He sat down next to me and we watched her sleep for a few more minutes before returning to bed.

Lizzie grew fast, as babies tend to do. Before we knew it she was rolling and scooting around the floor. She said her first word: No! Other words quickly followed, but that remained one of her favorites for a long time. She started to crawl and walk. Before we knew it we were approaching her first birthday.

It was hard on me thinking of Lizzie turning one. I wasn't entirely ready to let go of her being a baby. It had taken us so long to have a baby and now she wouldn't be a baby anymore. Mike and I wanted more children, but we both felt like Lizzie would probably end up being our only child. So I felt all the more desire to hold onto her being a baby a little longer.

Approaching Lizzie's first birthday I felt a huge mix of emotions and I desperately needed something to distract me. I did what any mom would do; I planned a huge first birthday party, complete with a circus theme.

There was a clown, a juggler, a cake shaped to look like a big red and white circus tent. We had circus themed foods, like popcorn and cotton candy, and lots of games. Lizzie slept through most of it.

But we were surrounded by friends and family. All the kids there had a great time. And Lizzie managed to wake up from her nap long enough to open some presents and smear cake all over her hair and dress.

That evening, after the party was over, we put Lizzie down for the night. Mike settled on the couch in front of the television to watch a sporting event of some sort and I pulled out another envelope: The Day Your Baby Turns One.

Dear Anna,

A baby's first birthday comes with mixed emotions: on one side of things you love watching your little one grow and develop, but at the same time you want so badly to hold onto how they are now. Time moves too fast. It's okay to feel a little sad that your baby is growing up; all moms do.

It's not always easy watching kids grow up. One of the hardest things about kids getting older is that it seems the older they get the harder it is to protect them. When your child is little a few socket covers and a baby gate and you feel like you can keep them from getting hurt, but sooner or later you realize that they are going to experience disappointment and failure. Life won't be perfect for them, just like I couldn't make it perfect for you.

The job of a parent is not to protect their child from hurt and disappointment. The job of a parent is to help a child learn how to endure whatever they may have to experience. Be encouraging. Teach your child to keep trying. I know you may be thinking that your child is only one, but you'll be surprised by how fast they grow and how soon you'll find yourself wanting to swoop in and protect them from the world.

Being a mom isn't an easy job. The bumps and bruises of a toddler are just the beginning. Before you know it you'll be sending them off to school, your heart breaking a little as they wave goodbye.

Tell your child how much their grandma loves them. I love you, my Anna.

-Mom

Chapter 14

Life went on as it tends to do, at times the days seemed to crawl by and yet the years seemed to fly. Lizzie started school. By then Mike and I had accepted that she would be an only child and with her gone all day, I started working again; only part-time while she was at school. I was still there when she got home from school and I enjoyed creating memories with her.

Lizzie would come home from school every day and sit at the counter and help me cook dinner. She'd tell me about her day. She'd tell me all about her friends. I loved these moments. They reminded me so much of my own childhood. And as she grew Lizzie reminded me of my mom more and more; her eyes had remained pale blue and she had gotten my mom's curly hair, too.

With Mike and me both working we realized that we could actually build a new house now. But as we talked about it, we decided that we just couldn't leave this house. My mom had been right; it wasn't just a house anymore. It was the house that we'd brought Lizzie home to when she was born and the house where she'd taken her first steps. It was our home and we decided to stay.

Life seemed to be going well, then one day the phone rang. It was my aunt; my dad was in the hospital. Mike left work and picked me up. We pulled Lizzie out of school and we made the two hour drive to the hospital. The drive seemed longer than I remembered and I found myself trying to will the car to go faster.

When we finally got to the hospital my aunt met me in the waiting room, along with some other family members. She explained that my dad had apparently had a stroke, but that the doctors said it had only been a minor stroke and that he'd be fine.

My aunt told me the room number and I went to see my Dad. Lizzie insisted on seeing Grandpa, too. At first I wanted to tell her no, to keep her from seeing him this way. But she was so insistent, so Mike and Lizzie ended up coming with me.

When I walked into the room I was immediately struck by all the machines and all the wires and tubes that connected them to my dad. Then I looked at my dad and he was still all smiles.

"Hey, kiddo! Did you bring Grandpa a present?"

Lizzie giggled, "No! You're the Grandpa, you're the one who brings the presents."

I smiled, "Lizzie, Grandpa doesn't have a present for you this time."

"Oh, no?" asked my dad, reaching for something on his side table, "I had Aunt Deb grab these because I knew you'd be coming." He handed Lizzie a big bag of candy.

"Thank you, Grandpa," she said hugging him. He winced a little as she squeezed.

We sat and visited for a while. Dad tried to reassure me that he was fine and that he'd be up and about in no time, but something was different. I had trouble putting my finger on it at the time, but looking back I realized that he actually seemed better and happier than he'd been in a long time. It seemed funny to find myself enjoying the visit so much, considering the circumstances.

After a while, a nurse poked her head in and let us know that visiting hours would be ending soon. We said our goodbyes.

I paused at the door, "I love you, Daddy." He gave me a big smile, "Love you too."

I walked back to his bed and gave him a big hug. I held on, I guess because a part of me knew what was coming.

We went back to my dad's house to stay the

night, just to be close to the hospital. The next morning I woke up early to the sound of my cell phone ringing. It was the hospital. My dad had apparently had another stroke in the middle of the night. They had tried everything they could. He didn't make it.

I hung up the phone. I had always thought that losing my mom was hard because I had lost her so early. I thought that if I had more time with her that losing her would have somehow been easier. Losing my dad I realized that no matter how much time you have with a person, when they leave it's always too soon for the ones they leave behind.

I called my Aunt Deb and asked her to make phone calls to the rest of the family. I spent the day making funeral arrangements. Family and friends dropped by to offer help and support.

The funeral wouldn't be for a few days and I had taken care of the things that needed to be done, so that evening we drove home. With my dad gone, I just wanted to go home; to our home. It was late when we pulled up to the house. Mike pulled a sleeping Lizzie from the car and laid her down in her bed.

I went to our bedroom, got down the jewelry box and pulled out an envelope that I had been dreading. As I unfolded the letter a smaller page fell to the floor. I picked it up. Folded inside the letter from my mother was this note from my dad:

Dear Anna,

I just wanted to include a note to tell you how much I love you. I miss you already, sweetheart. Just remember that I am with your mom now and we are happy together. I love you forever.

-Dad

I held the note and read it over and over again. I cried until I couldn't see well enough to read it anymore.

After I had gotten a hold of myself, I finally set down the note from my dad and picked up the letter: The Day Your Dad Passes Away.

Dear Anna,

I am so sorry that you have to go through this kind of pain again. I hope you had a long time with your dad before this day came. Remember the time that you spent with your dad. Think of all the great memories that you had with him. Please don't forget those times, even though it may be painful to remember at first.

I know that for you this day will be filled with loss and sadness, but at the same time, this is a day that your dad and I have been looking forward to. We're together again. It may be selfish of me, but I am excited to be with your dad again whenever this day may come.

Anna, I love you so much. I miss you. Thank you for taking care of your dad for me.

-Mom

Chapter 15

More years passed. There were other letters here and there. Lizzie got older and went from Elementary School to Middle School. Life got busy, but I still took time now and then to sit in the garden and talk to my mom and my dad.

It was a few days after Lizzie's fourteenth birthday that I found myself sitting in the doctor's office, staring at my doctor, trying to absorb what she was telling me. "What do you mean a lump?" I asked.

"It may be nothing," she said, "but I just want to do a biopsy and make sure."

My head felt like it was spinning. I couldn't believe what she was saying. I started running through all the worst-case-scenarios in my mind. The sample was taken and sent to be tested. It was a Friday, so the doctor promised to get back to me with results after the weekend.

I somehow managed to drive home. I told Mike about what had happened. We spent the weekend running over all the "what-ifs". He tried to reassure me that everything was going to be fine. "I'm sure it's nothing. She's just being cautious. No matter what happens we'll get through this."

It was the longest few days of my entire life. I thought about my mom. I thought about Lizzie and about how young she was; almost as young as I'd been. I prepared myself for the worst.

Monday came and I kept myself busy around the house, waiting for a call from the doctor. Finally the phone rang. The doctor reassured me that everything came back normal and there was nothing to worry about. I got off the phone and called Mike at work. I sat down at the table and cried tears of relief and joy.

I pulled out a piece of paper and a pen and sat down. This had turned out to be nothing, but the weekend had gotten me thinking. What if I did die? What would Lizzie have of me? My mother had been lucky enough to know that her time was short, but what if she had just passed away suddenly? How much harder would my life have been if I hadn't had the letters? I picked up the pen and began writing: Dear Lizzie.

Gradually I wrote a whole box of letters to Lizzie. Each envelope is labeled the same as the ones that my mom gave me: The Day You Turn Sixteen; The Day You Graduate from High School; The Day You Get Married. I've already lived to see her open and read some of these letters and I hope that I get to watch her read many more. But the box is there, full of a lifetime of wisdom and experience, and that gives me some peace of mind. No matter what happens I will always be there for her, just like my mom was there for me.

ABOUT THE AUTHOR

Jami Brookes Berry was born and raised in Utah and now lives there as a stay at home mother of two young girls. In addition to writing, she enjoys music, photography and spending time with her family.

Made in the USA
San Bernardino, CA
30 November 2013